The Frog Prince

My 1st Classic Story

a retelling of the Grimms' fairy tale

by Eric Blair

illustrated by Todd Ouren

PICTURE WINDOW BOOKS
a capstone imprint

My First Classic Story is published by Picture Window Books
A Capstone Imprint
151 Good Counsel Drive, P.O. Box 669
Mankato, Minnesota 56002
www.capstonepub.com

Library of Congress Cataloging-in-Publication Data
Blair, Eric.
The frog prince : a retelling of the Grimms' fairy tale
retold by Eric Blair ; illustrated by Todd Ouren.
p. cm. — (My first classic story)
Summary: An easy-to-read retelling of the classic tale
of a beautiful princess who makes a promise to a frog
which she does not intend to keep.
ISBN 978-1-4048-6083-4 (library binding)
[1. Fairy tales. 2. Folklore—Germany.] I. Ouren, Todd, ill.
II. Grimm, Jacob, 1785-1863. III. Grimm, Wilhelm, 1786-1859.
IV. Frog prince. English. V. Title.
PZ8.B5688Fr 2011
398.2—dc22
[E]   2010003624

Art Director: Kay Fraser
Graphic Designer: Emily Harris

The story of *The Frog Prince* has been passed down for generations. There are many versions of the story. The following tale is a retelling of the original version. While the story has been cut for length and level, the basic elements of the classic tale remain.

Once upon a time, there was a king with many daughters. The youngest daughter was the most beautiful.

The young princess had a golden ball.
It was her favorite toy.

By the forest, there was a deep well. The princess would go near the well and play with her golden ball.

One day, the ball landed in the well.
The princess started to cry.

"Why are you crying?" a frog asked.

"I lost my golden ball in the well,"
the princess said.

"What will you give me if I get your ball?" the frog asked.

"Whatever you want," the princess said.

"Let me be your friend," the frog said.

The princess agreed. But the princess wasn't telling the truth.

She was thinking, *This frog is silly.*
How could a frog ever have a human
for a friend?

The frog dived into the well. He quickly returned with the golden ball.

The princess picked up the ball and
quickly ran away.

The next day, the princess was at the dinner table with her father, the king. There was a knock on the door.

The princess ran to see who was at the door. When she saw the frog, she slammed the door in his face.

"Who was that?" he asked.

"It's just an ugly frog," she said.

The princess told her father about the ball, the frog, and the promise she had made.

The king said, "When you make a promise, you must keep it. Let him in."

The princess did as her father ordered.

"Pick me up, and put me on your chair," the frog said. Again, the king made the princess do it.

21

"Push your plate closer so we can eat together," the frog said.

The princess did what the frog asked, but she didn't like it.

When the frog was done eating, he said,
"I'm tired. Take me to your bedroom."

The princess began to cry. Her father became angry. "When someone helps you and you have made a promise, you must keep it," the king said.

The princess carefully picked up the frog.
She carried him upstairs to her bedroom.

The princess put the frog on the floor in
her bedroom. She crawled into her bed
and turned off the light.

"I'm tired, and I want to go to sleep. Lift me up, or I'll tell your father," said the frog.

The princess became angry. She picked up the frog and threw him against the wall as hard as she could.

"There, you ugly frog! Now you'll sleep,"
she said.

When he dropped to the floor, the frog turned into a handsome prince. He told the princess a wicked witch had cast a spell on him. She had broken the spell!

The princess let the prince become her dearest friend and husband. They lived happily ever after.

The End